# The Next Noise Is Our Hearts

Kathleen Willard

Books may be purchased in quantity and/or special sales by contacting the publisher. All inquiries related to such matters should be addressed to:

Middle Creek Publishing & Audio
9161 Pueblo Mountain Park Road
Beulah, CO 81023
editor@middlecreekpublishing.com
(719) 369-9050

First Paperback Edition, 2024
ISBN: 978-1-957483-24-5
Cover Art: Johanna Mueller
Cover Design: Stephen Willard

# The Next Noise Is Our Hearts

Kathleen Willard

Middle Creek Publishing & Audio
Beulah, CO   USA

# Table of Contents

## Megafauna

## Paradise

For Emmit Carico & Lucy Carico

# Utopia

# Utopia

A small boy rocks his body back and forth
as he sings a song that names the planets
in their correct order from the sun
to the outermost edges of our solar system
with uncanny precision and delights
in their descriptors—a mnemonic device.
He is especially pleased when he belts
out the lyrics like a singer in a rock band:
*Jupiter is a big, big, big gaseous planet.*
And he sways, thrilled at the beauty of the words,
hearing the music of the spheres,
in awe of the planets in our solar system
suspended, as if by magic, in a dark sea of space.
He will be happy to share the names of every species,
all eighteen, of penguins on the planet and you will learn
what country they live in, not all on Antarctica,
a fact that shocks me.
For an entire year, this child, during his daily kindergarten
writing workshop wrote of bees, every entry
fact after fact after fact and read his findings,
a master already of the kingdom of bees,
to his class. He is a member of an imaginary
hive of bees that lives in his bedroom full-time
and sometimes the bees swarm
and his mother, complicit in this universe,
opens the front door of the house
so the queen bee can lead her subjects to a new home.

After he stops singing, I ask,
*What's your favorite planet?*
And he looks at me as if I am imbecile,
as if I wasn't listening.
*Earth*, he answers. Stunned
I don't have access to this simple fact.
*Because we live here.*

# Renovation of the Human Race

## I.

She was an absentee hair whitened torn

and disheveled, a recent refugee from the underworld

clutching a basket of sacred frogs.

Vulnerable to the soft morning sun,

a shiny microdot, she was dumbstruck

with grief as the single eyewitness to caverns of torsos,

the stockpile of blue feathers from birds

driven to extinction.

Her recent dark habitat offered no comfort,

only an opaque and hastened her propensity

for shadows, her affection for the schools

of blind albino fish.

Imagine her relief when confronted by minarets of mountains,

and the two rivers called her to prayer.

The world sutured, animated,

 pulsates with this chaos of colors.

The world besieged by autumn.

## II.

My optics, my feral eyes fail to quantify temporary vixens

scarcely able to undo their perjury, to name the guilty,

to resurrect the dead.

Flying beneath the patriarchy, their testimony incoherent.

They are nothing but imposters disguising

themselves as transient fishes.

When in truth they are the next in succession, royalty really

ready to ship out ignoring their fatal addiction to sex.

While amicable at first, they steered their regatta

between the constellations and the house of the winds.

What in our arsenal could prepare us for this carnage?

All we can do is push dead bodies back into the waves,

bear witness to the morbid spectacle and return to our sail yards,

our factories of looms, and do our best to forget,

but atrocity rarely remains secret. The stories clamor

out of our throats as requiems honoring all extinctions

and ruptures.

**III.**

Explain, please

our quixotic interest in darkness, our exposé clamors

for a bit of clarity concerning the odd movement of parasites

and serial killers promoted

to the column marked heroes.

The world is spinning bitter, and there is glory

in the abundance of blood and splatter. What's

happening to the chambers of our bodies,

the reliquaries for our hearts?  Our larynxes

are in remission and we have long ago adjusted

to silence, no one speaking out, our hands dry-docked

and stacked up in rafters. And the certainty of circumcision

hastens ghosts of tigers, the last songs of the lynx.

## IV.

We applaud the nature of prodigies

their broad jaws, their shoulders spawning fins

near an altar of maples, cluttered with reliquaries.

I have tamed all

carnivorous things, freeing each from its

corporeal body to walk undocumented

to the dark side of the moon.

The naturalists absent, who missed

the annual rapture of the abstract moths,

rush to measure with their crude instruments

the apertures of the sky. Lacerated, jubilant

the echoes of the dead reach even here.

## V.

The world is carnivorous.

Our alma maters must be asylums

why else applaud each violation?

The men obsessed with our animus,

our absolutes as we dress ourselves

in furious turbans with no trepidation

of this fraudulent behavior. We dismiss

whispers of lovers, intent instead

on the cynical. Ministers ignore

the outbreak of amputees, sweep

maimed members into barrels

of biohazards. How cavalier

we have all become sending our most beautiful

to battle cleaving to the mythos of the Cold

War, the world abundant with bombardiers,

with terrorists rapt in propaganda.

We are all embedded, riding atop tanks.

**VI.**

Inside the solarium, all things begin with inertia

a sort of resistance, as with the river eroding

outcroppings of rocks.  Here, a sense

of the very vertigo familiar to the irregular sun.

The stars, have you noticed, move farther away

from our planets fatigued by centuries of

sinister assertions, our blood pulsating

to the speed of light.  We have been abandoned

and left to distrust innumerable theories

of everything, even the certainty of carbon dating,

the nuances of evolution, and left with an abundance

of afterimages of the bleak.

## VII.

This was not the accustomed slaughter

clutching their school reports about the planets.

Cue, Saturn. Cue, the stroke of the sword across

their bird-thin necks. The groans of heaven

grow vulgar, skewer the relatives of ingenious wolves.

They trespass on white marble, violating

the recesses of our brains and igniting spectral

concussions with the blasts of their bullets,

their crude bomb denotations overfilling rivers

with plagues of bees.

                           Their forte dissonance

wrapping their faces in the shawls

of useless manifestos. So this is jihad,

the holy war to silence the innocent to the oblique

and turn their beautiful bodies to remarkable

whiteness.  Their dogma declares children infidels,

their fierce dreams a crime against the state.

In the teahouses, future assassins diagram

covert operations in the dirt, designate

which hand will hold the gun to the temple

of the girl. The sky fills with a reservoir of blood.

There will never be enough surgeons to suture

our wounds.

## VIII.

In safe neighborhoods young

boys ambushed by centaurs

with no patience for sissies

are exiled into mountains

to learn stories from trees

but their bodies calculated

are alternatives to ordnance

now fodder for delusional generals.

On command, breathtakingly beautiful boys

charge into a barrage

of spears and arrows undaunted, invincible.

Why do stories always end this way?

Ante up, as always, too many tyrants

ignore the chaos of children begging

for mercy. We flee into ancient temples

in search of atonement, one vibrato,

one single word from beyond the grave.

Fumigate, and forget the season's atrocities

as we are all servile to vectors of violence

as our voices grow hoarse and atrophy.

## IX.

First, the low song of winds, an orbit of insects
our lips mouth warnings silenced by the din
while mountains of dust opaque the sky.
Our irascible house lacquered by the veil
of locusts, our bodies instantly exsanguinated,
nullify, and the dark bits of our hearts
nourish the starving soil.
Our windows curtained by greedy crows
and invocations and infinite votives call on
the Intersession of the Saints, the vapid promises
to help the poor, treated as vagrants,
and ultimately unheeded, unheard.
All our household gods spit on our ostentatious
altars as we failed to notice the slippage
of stars from the heavens now cradled
by branches of agitated oaks.
It is much too late to call in the counterinsurgents,
to stockpile water.

## X.

I was served a plate of tongues

thick worms silent and arranged

in a circle inching off edges of porcelain

moist oysters almost and still

guns turmoil: they are meat grinders.

Autopsies confirm the obvious—

our new grim, small children

churn and liquefy and days grow darker.

Outrage & hymns

off-key at candlelight vigils,

afterthoughts & apologies,

as if to honor some constellation missed

by every astronomer for centuries.

Our one night honorarium

and then back, barricaded in gated communities still in awe

of access to our many automatics.

Our fingers galvanized

polishing stocks and barrels,

trigger-happy and ready

to protect. The momentary outrage

stilled, our arsenals unsurrendered.

## XI.

We clothe ourselves in jackets of glass

and skirts made from snips of tin and barbwire

aligned to the sun's cruel gaze

sacrosanct and parched.

This is the stance of the next martyr

attentive in our atonement.

We rely on the infinity of rosaries

scattered into the winds

and the sky punctuated with horsetail clouds.

Our SOS insignificant

unheard by a single soul.

Unsure of the requirements

to stave off thirst, we hear bitter news

the nectar to revive bees

hardened into stone.

Our cargoes will be raffled

once the ship completes

its transatlantic crossing

and dismiss rumors

our futile compass

refuses to point

to the North Star

our exodus delayed.

The angry sandstorm

gallops over the hills.

We wince as wind rips out our eyes.

# The Next Noise Is Our Hearts

## Sketches Towards a Libretto

### (fig. #1)

And now the last breath and the next crescendo.
One can barely discern the rebellion.

Clocks overhear, and the lilies begin.
Rhetoric calligraphy commences the arousal and the crows.

Now, the celebrity of weapons opens the overture of tanks.
The faint trees migrate. Stage left, as though an opera,

the noise overshadows slim rents in our hearts,
the dirges oversee dowagers and children of dust. Stones hum.

The vesper of whispers in meadows retaliate, begin
to leave and take widows, the walls, and the dead.

Constellations of the next rigor mortis launch
while outside, a body count of hands parades.

### (fig. # 2)

Commence the weapons and the stones hum left.
The dust begins rebellions.
The faint opera of calligraphy and the crows leave

the dead overshadowing
slim rents of arousal and rhetoric.
Breath, and the next noise is our hearts.

One barely discerns dirges from the overture of rigor mortis
and outside the next tank parade.

And then, the crescendo and the last trees migrate.
Stage, and launch the dowager's children and roll
the body count, the constellations of clocks,
the whispers in meadows.

Now, the celebrity of widows, walls and lilies overhear.

**(fig. #3)**

A parade of hands rolls through our opera of tanks.
Noise overshadows children, slim walls and the dead commence.
Widows and dowagers of dust hum, uprising the stones.

Stage left, now the celebrity of noise opens
rents in our hearts. Breath, and the next weapons migrate,
the next rigor mortis.

Clocks overhear dirges from faint trees.
The leave-taking and the meadows retaliate
their declarations.

One can barely discern the rebellion of the skies,
the overture of lilies begins outside constellations
of rhetoric, the body count calligraphy.

Crescendo and a vesper of whispers,
arousal and the crows
oversee and then, the next launch.

# The Colony

## Hooves & Trout

You taught me to recognize the trees with certainty
to feel bark and decode elm, know birch, declare maple.
Early in our lives we walked into the forest
and you looked down said *deer trail*,
recognizing the glance of their hooves
the almost-slight curves, almost obelisks,
and followed traces of broken twigs,
of willows grazed to their resting place,
the tall grass molded by curled bodies.
And banged on the riverbank
arousing sleeping trout.


And he insisted, *prepare*, the world ablaze
with astonishment and up the trail the air alive,
we chanced on a migration
of butterflies, a species unknown to us,
thousands and thousands hanging on every branch
of every tree, opening and closing their wings,
their tiny flags, the many pages of miniature books.

## Wasps & Windfalls

Like a mirror, or miracle, the summer's done
with the last hum of the honeybee. The world
relieved as the heat cools, the orchard obese
with plums paper wasps drunk-burrow
into ripe flesh. Still, winter is almost fictitious
and fumbles, stuns, and fails to notice
the last lift of geese on the pond or the trout
frazzled underneath a thin membrane of ice.

Windfalls ferment sustenance for our backyard
fox. I don't understand where summer went,
how our errant ferns yellowed, their fringed edges
browning. How the days quicken, now ash-filled,
now the color of dust.

## Livable Equilibrium

Naysayers ignore the data and the dirge and do not interrogate
the term livable equilibrium all a climate scientist
predicts is left.  He turns his sights to clouds
and cannot look the reporter in the eye.
The world's unraveling and no sleight of hand
or armada can lead us out of this maze. It's real.
What does it mean? A kaleidoscope
of charts tutors us how to do the math,
and computer models predict
what's next, but we have no idea
about the reality of the world we will live in,
or if the procedures to combat incineration or inundation
will be enacted and all I can think is *how soon will honeybees*
*cease to gather nectar and feed us?*
For now, the plants and creatures
first imperiled by incineration lack sex appeal.

Yes, we can do without an endemic rodent
on a cay, a blue butterfly on the mountains
of Spain, but what of the honeybee?

## The Last Outpost of the Some Honey Bees

But what of the honey bees? The cohort
drinks from my backyard fountain, a way station
between hive and flower. Their magic interaction
between sun and bloom render
nectar and pollen into sweetness
all tongues savor.
Small prophets proclaim us monsters
and forage for blooms trek
from aromatic fields and orchards
and to their hive twenty-five thousand times
for every pound of honey
then spin, sun-golden fanning their wings
*into the prime matter, the sweetness of earth*
*that resides naturally in growing things.* The hinge
of one-third of everything we eat.

The essence of two million flowers are spun sun
into golden and honey on tongues
spurs lovers to birth
gods and goddesses and humans.
The queen's chemicals,
the queen's pheromones, the queen instigates
and oversees the fate of the hungry
foretelling famine.
The countdown commences:
seven species of bees fly onto the endangered species list
and *forty percent of all invertebrate pollinators*
*face extinction.*

## Once Royalty

*Forty percent of all invertebrate pollinators*
*face extinction* and seven species
of Hawaiian yellow-faced bees
move one step closer, the new inductees
to the endangered species list. The wasp look-alikes
with branched plumage hairs and elongated thorax
reached Hawaii on its own one original colonist
imploded to 63 endemic species flew over the Pacific,
unencumbered, and did not piggyback on other creatures.
Solitary aviators
navigated thousands of miles of open sea,
making landfall on this archipelago.
The gold mark on the male bee's forehead
like a third eye
or a smear of ashes
our parish priest dispenses
before Lent.
Once abundant, once royalty of coastlines
and rulers over sub alpine slopes of Mauna Kea,
and now stealth insects rarely seen.

*The bees are a lot worse off than we thought.*
Their slick, shiny bodies, speed demons
fly past humans, leaving trails of sound
and disappearing under a cloak of invisibility—
resisting census.

Entomologists engineer
bee nest boxes, as *genus Hylaeus* forgoes hives for cavities
in coral washed ashore or hollow stems of coastal plants.
Their hypothesis:
installations of artificial homesteads may encourage mating,
but this desperate architecture is easily outwitted
by rising seas and storms surges.

# Landscape with Infestation

And so, the new tableau.
*The trees have no heart*, a scientist said.
*No circulatory system, no savior from drought,*
*no savior from infestation.* Stands of certain
conifers have no mechanism to stay
the stymied xylem or all embolisms
or resistance against swarms of tiny cannibals
riding the winds, this silent invasion,
an epidemic assured.
Ips and pine bark beetles—we are all blind
to their procedures of bore and breed,
the insect explosion inside of offspring gnaw
and chisel out the core of tree,
murders all systems of survival.
The mountains brown overnight
and there is nothing to be done.
The forest is a stand of cadavers,
decomposing. The demise of
several species is a certainty.
The trees will stop breathing
and beetles in their exoskeletons
are invincible architects
of the new world.

# Dear Lucy—

Today, I am thinking about your migration.
How you cast off every morning, always in motion.
You move through the world dancing, flapping your arms,
leaping into air hoping for new winds,
spinning on your toes to conjure levitation.
Honing in on your pivot point, you embrace the moment
your body lightens.

I am sure, at five, you have traveled the distance
from Central America to southern Canada,
the migratory path of monarch butterfly.
For you look to the clouds mapping out maneuvers
between cumulus and cirrus ready
to join their journey as they fill the sky orange
and travel into the blue.

At the butterfly pavilion, you stilled,
and painted ladies and monarchs welcomed
you by flying over your head and landing only on your dress,
claiming you as kin.

And together we learned the exact location monarchs winter over.
Deep in the jungle, they embrace and encase every tree
and wait for the sun to dry their wings, their subtle sounds
of flight mimics a waterfall.

How can I tell her the days of her monarchs and their migrations
are numbered? Their mortality rate accelerating
at breakneck speed and sooner than we think,
she will have to fathom a world
where monarchs no longer visit backyards.

# Western Interior Seaway

# Cirque & Sky

Eager stowaway ready to board any sailing ship,
I disembark on a different shore,
escape the enslavement of a house.

Yes, our cottonwoods bleed branches in hot winds,
but I could care less witchgrass chokes
yellow daylilies once so lovingly planted.
I long ago abandoned the garden that anchored,

enthralled instead by the genius
of sky, point my camera
into clouds intent on enlarging my orbit,
resume study of my archive

of tin globes and old maps highlighting
the routes of barbarians and Arctic explorers,
culling provision lists,
noting their grand intentions.

In this decade, I long for pristine landscapes,
for an incognito, to be sequestered
in a secret cirque blushing alpine flowers,
their almost microscopic petals barely
span my fingertips.
Here, elk have never heard a human voice.

## Kestrels & Western Interior Seaway

Once, Colorado was an inland ocean alive with prehistoric fish
inundated by water drowning the modern landscape,
the continent split in two and incomprehensible
creatures swam between mountains and mesas

miles above our heads and teemed with monstrous
fish and their terrible teeth. Aquatic forests waved in the current.
We walk the former ocean floor and scatter fossils
like a galaxy of stars. Scramble the scree of rocks

for a better view of our ocean of mesas marked and measured
by Steamboat Rock, a monolith.
Kestrels dive bomb us, fly to the perfect apex,
achieve a precise angle,
turn earthward, wings tight by their sides,

their feathers reverb in the wind. Meanwhile,
rock outcroppings rise like a city on either side of us,
encrusted with evidence of eons of aquatic life.
And you, overturned stone after stone
confident somewhere in random

piles of limestone, you would unearth a fossil
until one stone imprinted with tiny traces
of plant life emerges,
the same pattern repeating etched on rock
with an organism, a stoic token of the once-was world.

## Uravan, Colorado

Fenced off, nine miles inside barbed wire,
and signs warning of radioactivity and *keep out*
*enter at your own risk*, the site closed for all eternity,
after the two hundred and sixty buildings shredded
and buried, all trees demolished, all
ripped apart with hydraulic shears
even the soil buried in a repository built
to endure the worst storms imaginable in the next
thousand years—the town a player in the nuclear
race. *We are not afraid of uranium here*, the widows say
and take rock samples of uranium from their knickknack
shelves part of their décor and share
the black and white photos of Uravan in its heyday:
their children sliding down hills of radioactive tailings,
used also to lay water pipes, to amend garden soil;
the class pictures in front of the elementary school
and recreation center; the evenings at the Uranium
Drive-in Movie Theatre
near the place where yellowcake was milled,
the soon-to-be enriched material, a necessary
ingredient for the first atomic bomb.
The acceptable risk: lungs crystallizing
from cancer, maybe from working deep
in the earth, maybe from smoking,
maybe from the uranium, the radium,
the vanadium coaxed from orange
and neon yellow buttes and quiet mesas.

## Landscape with Wildfire

The sky burns orange brocade
smears clouds surreal
singes canyons beyond recognition
a hysteric dancing
from treetop to treetop chars
everything in its wake. So,
this is the apocalypse
no longer theoretical.
Every large and small
living thing stampedes to safety~
wrens and honeybees
unable to outrun insistent heat.
Spiders spin
their last webs
as ash avalanches from the sky
and shrouds our house. The invisible
census of the soon incinerated
commences, impossible
to complete. Flames jump
fire breaks and even the river
advances as the canyon quivers
and overheats and arroyos crumble.
Hotshot crews cannot contain the inferno.
The news stuns us as the fire's heat
spawns its own clouds and fallout.
The air sizzles
the wall of smoke marches through the city
and the fire whirls in the forest
births tornadoes of flames.

## South Platte River, Benzene Spill

Benzene, benign, benevolent at the turn of the last century
once an ingredient in men's aftershave,
nicknamed frankincense of Java for its seductive smell,
attractive to the opposite sex,
in the recipe for soda, in the formulary for Sanka.
Benzene once stocked in quart cans in hardware stores,
handled by students measuring out millimeters
for science experiments.
And yes, the refinery
fell short, spilling enough carcinogens to fill an Olympic-size pool
into a silence until a fly fisherman on the South Platte
gagged on the smell of oily sheen
the weird, milky sludge clogged
upswells and mircocurrents
stilling some sixty carp
alive, but not very active and wrote a blog.
Benzene, so carcinogenic,
so regulated, a flume fans out
and seeps into groundwater
and yes, Suncor fell short of its commitment
to the city and only after the blog went viral
*my flies smelled like gas, my hands smelled like gas*
did they send a cavalry of cleanup crews
resplendent in white
biohazard suits skimming the water.

# Fracking

These are our apparitions: the sky gleans towards gray,
the mouths of caves filled with quartz call.

How long before we are all fluent in earth,
our scarring stops? In an office an engineer

imagines molecules deep past aquifers
speaks combustion and churns engines and blasts

sand and benzene near the earth's core
unloosens eons of errant natural gas dormant

underneath Pawnee Grasslands, an oily ocean
the size of Saudi Arabia still and docile waits

underneath the fossil beds of mastodons
and eohippus, the knee-high horses,

first to run wild on the prairie,
underneath everyone's water source,

underneath artifacts and evidence of prehistoric
campsites of Folsom man, the Paleo-Indian inhabitants

from 12,000 years ago
underneath the final outpost

of the Colorado butterfly plant imperiled globally
—the ocean awaits to be split open

with mobile steel girders and slamming
concrete sleeves and fallible

into the deepest recesses of rock to pipe
toxic concoctions by roustabouts overworked

and now acrid aluminum air
irritates and fire streams from water faucets

in the nearby suburbs. The bonds
of our cells unhinge

unleashing old and new contagions
and cover ups the whole procedure

deemed safe while around
the clock earth cracks open,

we tinker with tectonic plates.

## West Wind & West Fire

We are all exiles
when it comes to fire
and failures at its domestication
and cannot fully comprehend
fire psychology and have never
come to terms with its feral nature
once fueled by oxygen
and its aria of relentless winds,
and once ignition of the brittle
forest occurs, all one can do is step
back and let the landscape sizzle
and send in futile battalions of young men
with backpacks and plastic jugs of gasoline,
chainsaws and axes
to dig miles of firebreaks with their pickaxes
and shovels.
In the West,
we brace for fire season,
our new fifth season,
when our world singes
and brittles,
and come to terms
with waves and waves of flames
and fire sprinting over
too many acres to contain
and watch how fire breeds tornadoes
of flames spiraling up past fourteeners,
past even clouds,
and collapses on ground miles from its origin,
conquering new territory.
The blaze explodes and travels
from treetop to treetop
out of our reach.
It eviscerates ponderosa pine
and spruce into a phalanx of black spikes
and the dark bark of trees paints a new landscape of the West
with ash, the principal tint, the new mainstay
of the artist's palette.

## Out West, Water is Fickle

It rolls in and out of our lives,
so sleight of hand.
Drought never ends, only pauses,
a time-out for a few years and, returns.
We always act surprised.
As if, drought was a new catastrophe
we have no idea how to manage.
As if, the complex system of New Deal
dams and irrigation ditches
will change its personality.
As if, we can engineer all drought
into extinction.

Drought hibernates like bears.
Comes back, knocks
on our screen doors
and moves into our homesteads
like the black sheep
of the family fresh from drug rehab.
It pleads it needs just a few months
to get back on its feet
and sets up housekeeping on our sofas.

And we, who live in the West,
shocked weather cruelly turns against us
so fiercely, engage in an epidemic of mass amnesia.

Our crops shrivel. Our lawns brown and crackle.
Our suburban oasis recedes.
We litigate first dibs on snowmelt,
and sell our livestock below market value.
We speak of water capture and wish to incarcerate
the river flow from states downstream.

We take our losses once again
as aquifers wither and fail to comprehend
once they are gone, they are gone.
And this story is passed down from generation
to the generation without remedy or resolution.

## Sunset, Sangre de Cristo Mountains

A forest of wings! A forest of wings!
The valley sun-bloodied.
*The war was just over*
*and there was little to do but imagine.*
The herd of clouds shrouds
the mountains one cluster militant
spills down the pale valley
floor. Our abacus counts
the multitude of horses
and keeps track of many ways
to speak of love. Our tally
could fill a palazzo. Like mica,
the flock of turquoise reflects
light and flies into silvered
fields. Sagebrush seething.
I wonder how to fashion
bracelets of charms from the Milky Way.
Turn to my catalog of disorder,
sort new specimens collected
over the years. Devise in my dreams
a periodic table of agitation.
And became distracted
when the Earth tilted
away from light
and the sun dove into the dark sea.
Of course, the full moon rose
a bit akimbo, its arch barely
visible above the teeth
of mountain peaks
and spun overhead
into the theatre of stars.
The blue mountains turned
bloodred, a miracle
that brought conquistadors
to their knees.

# Megafauna

# Farewell, Sudan

I.
Swipe left, swipe right, a last ditch effort to be picked on Tinder
to find a perfect mate
for Sudan, the lone male northern white rhinoceros,
the only one on seven continents, a repugnant
armored car tank mash-up straining to be a loveable
creature in its pic. Recently rejected as a sex partner
by its two female zoo mates, its zookeepers resorted
to a dating app and declared Sudan
the World's Most Eligible Bachelor, looking
for another species of rhino somewhere to love him
and fundraise for his captive breeding program,
a desperate effort to abate his extinction.
His forefathers were coveted for their exquisite horns
ground into powder by apothecaries for headaches
and hallucinations, snakebites and demonic possession.
Coveted for luxury good
bragging rights of the bored ultra-rich
to be the first of their cadre
to sip whisky from rhino-horn cups
and fill curio shelves
with rhino-horn carvings,
their carcasses abandoned to hyenas
and vultures on the savanna. The app crashed,
a first for Tinder, as the world spasmed in horror,
breaking our hearts. At this writing,
only five northern white rhinos
alive on the planet, destined to be apparitions ghosted.

II.

The last male white rhino on the planet and destined
to be an apparition ghosted,
Sudan lived past his life expectancy,
his shelf life expired. On what day I care not to remember
or memorialize, his vet for decades euthanized him.
Once upon a time the infant rhino was exported
from the plains of Sudan,
to spend his life as an embellishment
in the Dvůr Králové Zoo in Czechoslovakia.
Its mission to experiment
with captive breeding to save
the northern white rhinos and outwit
the biology of extinction.
All lovers know stress obstructs desire
and lowers libido and displacement
from the African grasslands
to Czech winters disrupts
cues and what ever triggers
a creature to breed absent in the laboratory
and experiments to replicate mechanisms of nature
a failure. Some creatures perceive rain and begin breeding
and certain birds only mate when they can eat
conifer seeds and just like us,
there are particulars that seize us unexpectedly
and compel us to collide into each other with ferocity
which startles and what variables drive me
or any animal into this frenzy
remains mysterious.

# Captive Breeding

I.

What variables drives me or any animal into this frenzy
remains mysterious.
Why this holy grail of captive breeding?
Sudan and his harem repatriated to
Kenya, in Ol Pejeta in a laboratory,
a Hail Mary pass, a desperate effort
inside a conservancy, inside a secure laboratory,
inside two electric fences with four watch towers
with armed guards as protection from poachers.
Their horns the most valuable commodity on the planet.
Each rhinoceros assigned
a 24-hour body guard armed
with AK-47 and supplemented by
a heavily armed detachment of the Kenya Wildlife Service,
and a phalanx of fierce guard dogs and scientists
and veterinarians and humanitarians
all in a frenzy to save this species
if they could, in beakers, magnetically
stir the northern white rhino's semen into viable zygotes
provide the perfect environment for an embryo
to flourish and implant them in one of the last four females
once left on the planet, and now a surrogacy
the desired result, a population explosion,
a solution everyone who loves rhinoceroses
in a fierce fashion prays for.

II.

In a fierce fashion, I pray for a solution,
but if I was this creature, I would not welcome this intrusion,
and I am sure there would never be a stirring,
only a series of small stones and my molecules
resist transubstantiation, the alchemy
of producing an individual animal, a certain failure.
I would become a hermit with a caving heart,
unable to take one for the cause.
Each time my body rejects in vitro,
I turn my head away from my keepers
and face the corner of my enclosure.
Because genocide is not reversible
and once five, now four,
now two northern white rhinos are trace elements
of a species that thrived
since the Cretaceous period
in Sudan, in the Democratic Republic of the Congo,
in the Central African Republic, in Uganda.
How many misfires and miscarriages
would I endure to disprove their hopeful experiment?
Will they ever concoct the correct combination
of chemicals to trigger heat, altering my interior,
and create an ecosystem welcoming new life?

## On the *Exhibition of a Rhinoceros at Venice* by Pietro Longhi, 1751

Like the hippopotamus that lived
its entire life in a boxcar
in a sort of hybrid aquarium

travelling with a ragtag circus,
both creatures cajoled by spectators,
both creatures penned

and deemed freaks of nature,
trapped in diminished ecosystems,
imprisoned for thrill seekers.

A commodity, an oddity
feeding our need for dominion.
All caged creatures surrogates
for our secret sadomasochist thrills.

How did their captors lasso and transport
both behemoths from the rivers of Africa,
or from the forests of India?

Docile as house cats,
able to endure cramped spaces
and the throngs of

Venetians on their way to the last
orgy before Lent, white-masked,
black-robed, sequestered under
tricorn hats, anonymous.

The woman holds her ivory fan
in front of her,
like a subtle weapon
bored with your captivity.

It had been two centuries since Europeans
encountered a rhino, now Clara,
became an instant celebrity and sat for portraits across
the continent. Clara, a monolith, a mammoth,

a grotesque, thick-muscled and subdued.
In the painting, you refuse to face the viewer.

One day, I will read the learned
scholar Maffei's dissertation about you
against the backdrop of relentless bondage and slavery,

noting the atrocities,
querying about your survival.
And centuries later,

a circus came to my town
and set up their city of canvas tents
and I went to see the animals,

especially the elephants, only to encounter
a hippopotamus immersed in a boxcar aquarium.
The sides pushed down or opened up

like a garage door and behind the thick
glass in piss and shit-filled water,
a river horse filled

the entire perimeter
of a makeshift cage.
His round ears, gray-smooth skin,
stubby legs—bloated and bovine and beautiful.

And the crowd
shuffled by and the hippopotamus
stared back at us
with his small and weary and accusatory eyes.

## Bison, bison

*Here is an inexorable law of nature*
*to which there are no exceptions,*
*no wild species of bird or mammal,*
*reptile or fish can withstand*
*exploitation for commercial purposes.*

William T. Hornaday, master taxidermist,
The American Museum, 1889

### 1872

Everyone knows what happened to the bison.
How millions graced the Great Plains with their dignity,
their regal presence, of their task as epicenter of the ecosystem,
feeding the people, seeding the prairie,
and their speed of light extinction
expedited by the next get rich scheme of the West
and the marketplace of the East overly eager for bits of bison.

The bison became the last gold rush spawned
fortune hunters hellbent by new schemes
of striking it rich and the time of pioneers
waiting five days for herds of bison
to pass faded fast.

While customers in the East sat
in their debauched and decadent parlors,
for the arrival of boxcars filled with bison
tongues in brine, bison hides for the haute
couture coats, bison heads to display over mantlepieces
so the man of the house could pretend
he killed it.

Each person on the bison assembly line
of destruction akin to a serial killer,
their collective bloodlust guaranteed genocide.

So estranged from nature, the consumers
of bison could not imagine in their mind's eye,
the millions and millions and millions of bison
reduced to rotting carcasses littering the prairie.

## 2024

I am researching the decomposition of a body
of any living organism left to rot in the sun available to the elements.
I am thinking of aftermath.
I am thinking about disappearance.

I am thinking of 30 million megafauna disintegrating
on the Great Plains, their bodies speed bumps in gated communities.
How their purification altered the landscape
into a panorama of a battlefield.

How skin slippage and bloating liquified their bodies.
How the sky turned black with ravens.
How the packs of blissful wolves feasted
on bison they did not have to kill.
How the air filled with a putrid stench
heavy as a heat wave.

I am trying to to imagine the stench
of millions and millions and millions
of disemboweled bodies.

I am thinking of the West as boneyard, as catacomb, as killing field.

I am thinking of the parade of insects
also known as corpse fauna, rendering bison
to bone, the last bastion of their bodies
gleaming in the sun scattered like shattered fine bone china.

I am thinking what happens when their hearts
stop beating and their cells fail to function,
and when a bullet enters their lungs
and they fall to the ground

and battalions of skinners begin their work,
skinning hides from bodies and cutting out tongues.
How skinners become a factory disassembling
one animal after another animal all day long.

# Paradise

## Granite & Silver

However, our shadows.
However, mountains spit out
scaffolds of an abandoned mine still rich with silver
near the ruined city. Long ago, its saloons graced by oil paintings
of corpulent nudes denote a slow decay. Here minerals
shift in the mountain's interior and slender rivers
glide through sleeves of granite. We look at each other
as if it were the first time unveiling
ourselves in this ancient stand of aspens
gleaming gold in the late intaglio of the afternoon sun,
newlyweds despite
the decades, and breathe beautifully into each other's ears.
Some say mountains brim with lost treasure
and dim with a poor man's dissipated dreams. A horse
whinnies somewhere in the valley. Somewhere, granite
outcroppings beg for the first spit of snow.

## Red Willow & Red Fox

Each day is an encore. *Applaud*, he said.
As the stars grant night vision to the once-blind
and right before your very eyes, our horde of deer
rise from the underbrush of red willows, step out
from behind course-bark trees and announce—

Earnest dreams recede, regret lullabies us to sleep.
Bare branches rumple windows luring
us to the forest to witness
the yearly striptease, aspens undress,
but not before the grand finale.
Opulent leaves shimmer as hand mirrors signal SOS
to an indifferent sky.

Our days are filled with small miracles,
unnoticed, dismissed as hallucinations
brought on by inclement weather. How easy to ignore
the beautiful ordinary.

There, in the distant corner of my backyard,
a red fox steps out into the open.
How long has my garden been its habitat?

## Constellations & Fox

Just this revelation—

The morning begins glorious with the red fox
ravishing our backyard orchard, gorging on windfall apples
crisscrossing the *cul-de-sac*, a tame canine
pulling at the leash. What constellation did my fox discover
deep into the night, what clandestine comet
showers witnessed alongside astronomers of insomnia?
The fox slumbers under
our front porch, a strange member of our cat's pride,
and stalks our dreams, this dawn. The world floods
with eerie beauty: stellar jays croon,
the deer guards her speckled twins
grazing in our shrubbery.

How can they survive alpine winter,
the orange-vested hunters from out of state?
Migratory, they move to the high country
relying on camouflage
as the forest defoliates all around them.

## Aspen & Roots

The ocean of trees is our exaltation.
Aspens sigh their last yellow breath;
arrange themselves for autumn's
final autopsy. How clear the sky remains.
Thighs of mountains open,
fan out, in front of us, endlessly available.
Unostracized by proximity
to civilization, willows barbwire edges of the slow creek.
The world stills as we collide into each other.
I cannot get close enough to you.
So few enter this mile-high kingdom.
          Aghast, startled birds flee
and we hike well-worn elk trails
hidden by dynasties of aspen.
Scientists assert this stand of trees
is Earth's largest organism,
advancing root by root,
tendrils arching underneath
hard soil to conquer
territories on both sides
of the Continental Divide.

# The Meadow Calls

*for Gregory Crewdson*

The sudden explosion calls us.
Just bathed and in clean pajamas,
we ignore our mothers and raid
pristine pantries for mason jars,
take nails and hammer holes
for air on lids and hightail it to the meadow
liberated from the straightjacket
of suburbia. We run willy-nilly
into the dark fields zigzag lights pulsate,
the sky awash, ignore all stories of monsters
and wolves, of lurid creatures
beckoning us into the parallel world
even physicists postulate,
the alternate universe of fireflies.

Mesmerized by the inconstant light,
we swear allegiance to fireflies.
Their spell already cast. We run
into the dark under the stars,
under the moon, sprint
into the meadow with no battle plan,
no strategy to capture our prisoners of war,
pay no attention to landmarks
to guide us back home.

Our quarry: a continent of fireflies
to incarcerate a multitude
and condemn them to the hard labor
as night-lights in mason jars at our bedside
table, our single light source
until sunrise. We ignore
their desperate wish to escape
as they ram their small bodies
into the glass as they batter
their exoskeletons into extinction.
We are their executioners deaf to their dirge,
the tiny sounds of many wings beating glass.

## Heron & Rainstorms

Rumors of bear send many back to the city
and multitudes miss the blue heron crouched low by the river,
solo and silent, waiting for fish.
Before long, our hearing will be out of tune with water
and our offspring will grow tone deaf
to it rushing downstream.
Today the river is furious, overburdened by rainstorms
and is it always like this? As changeable as sky?
One morning the river turns indigo and silver,
fog rises breath above the cryptic surface,
then a smooth plate of glass inches downriver.
For me, forests are the perfect lyceum,
where pine branches sprout clipped wings of large angels,
their feathers of bark lay askew on the ground
and midstream, a quick flash of deer
sprints skittish out of view.
Yes, we are ambivalent about our expulsion
from the garden, but dry leaves rattle hymns to the wind—
clear evidence this is still Eden—
where everything happens for the very first time.

# There Was a Stranding

Let's dismiss the data, take down statistics, ignore
eyewitness accounts, say farewell to honeybees and pollinators,
all infinitesimal creatures, discard ecosystems,

and wait for the results. Six hundred stranded pilot
whales beach themselves, their sonar off-kilter,
the shoreline shifted,
their mass suicide defies scientific explanation.
Or how honeybees are flower-specific,
so many species depend on our cooperation.
Go figure, ecological changes occur
out of our line of sight, off-the-record
deep in forests or deep underwater.

Each small event a tick on the clock, the early
warning system ignored. Some heed the call
and travel to the New Zealand beach
to comfort a stranding of whales,
some too far gone to save
and encourage others back to the sea.
The breath from blowhole blasts,
and the futility of volunteers splashing seawater
on their beached bodies to counteract perishing,
follows comfort songs of teenage girls
keening for dying pilot whales. Declare
someone mourns their passing,
and they will not be alone
when they cross their last threshold.

## I Turn Animal

Altering my interior, my ecosystem, I turn animal—
frenzied, daily enraged
by the latest news: twenty-five species
destined to be ghosted
by the stroke of pen. The carnage continues
and their execution ensues despite millions of breaking hearts.
The decree begins: slow torture of habitats shrinking
and reduction of species to refugees
by machines of extinction.
And against the better judgment of scientists,
these twenty-five creatures are deemed
unworthy of even being added
to the endangered species list.

The first ever wholesale
rejection of Department of Interior
recommendations spotlights
the last days of the Pacific walrus,
the Bicknell's thrush,
the Barbour's map turtle,
the Florida Keys mole shrink,
the black-backed woodpecker,
the Big Blue Spring cave crayfish,
the Great Sand Dunes tiger beetle,
the San Felipe gambusia,
the eastern boreal toad,
Kirkland's snake,
14 Nevada springsnails—with
beautiful names—Bifid duct pyrg
and the Moapa pebblesnail.
Say farewell, our earth's autopsy begins
while forensics document the obvious.

# Bleaching

The desperate architecture outwitted by rising seas and storms surges.
Maps and 3D computer models
warn of cities destined to be inundated by surges that never recede
and this week I am assaulted
by photos of the Great Barrier Reef bleaching,
a phenomenon new to me, the whole ecosystem
ghosted and bone-bare, a skeleton of its former self
and gargantuan. I'm telling you with this revelation
I cannot sleep, a constant insomniac. No hope
the bleaching will ever be reversed and against such evidence,
a sector of society holds out climate change is a hoax,
a joke, and we are all fools, all alarmists as we watch
the Earth subtract and keep count of living organisms
getting zeroed out, until they are just taxidermy, dead,
dioramas, dormant, stilled and archived and labeled
in oak specimen cabinets in natural history museums
for future research and regard.
We are writing the obituary of the Earth.

# All Alabaster

We are writing the obituary of the Earth.
Our synapses cannot fathom the data of coral mortality
and divers surface from Great Barrier Reef reek of decay.
*Hard corals are dead and the flesh of animals*
*was decomposing and dripping off the reef structure.*
*The stench was on our skin.*
Divers discover crypts and catacombs
and document widespread bleaching of an organic structure
the size of Germany, all alabaster flashing
like lights of the Las Vegas Strip, a spectacle
visible from space.
And the eviction begins—
1625 species of fish,
130 species of sting rays and sharks, 30 species of whales,
and uncountable species of coral cannot survive
the warming ocean. The red slash on the satellite photographs
indicates coral bleaching
and bleeds like a mortal wound on the page,
the murder perpetuated, the Earth exsanguinates.
The heat from El Nino after El Nino trapped
by carbon and absorbed and boils ocean
and drastic measures no one quantifies
cannot stay the blood, while forensics point
to the obvious, we have lost the capacity
to be tender.

## Sky & Mount Antero

The sun silks mountains and shines granite

into skin of pale grey dolphin and breaching into the sky one

after another a school testing the new element exuberant

leaving water and leaping into air so expeditionary. The clouds

white-foamed waves, a border destabilizes between terra ferma

and ethereal air. Even the most miniscule

of elements break down and disperse

into the atmosphere. The spine

of fourteeners diminish as infinite sky

transubstantiates into infinite sea,

an alchemy imperceptible to the naked eye

## The Movement of the Stars

In my state, I should have perished,
but, I am going to end this heartbreaking narrative
and celebrate and use forbidden words
of *glorious* and *beauty* and *awe*
in the face of those bored by nature poetry,
who deem it redundant or lacking mystery.

What creatures fly together like a cloud,
flashing on radar, unknown entities
even to NORAD or meteorologists?

Simple, a painted ladies' storm surge:
a seventy-mile swath of butterflies
floods the Front Range occupies every flower
on prairies, in front yards,
on the upslope of the Rockies,
in pocket gardens of supermarket
parking lots. Weathermen target
ornithologists and entomologists
on social media to solve
the anomaly. The top story of the day:
*insects rarely produce*
*a coherent NORAD radar signal.*

The air afire with the prattle and bark
of red-tailed hawk fledglings nesting in my backyard.
All summer, they bicker at exhausted parents
like spoiled children of an upscale suburb.

Off a fern-edged trail, the prim garden of albino and ghostly
and translucent Indian pipes grow in the forest shadows. Stem to bloom
the plant's structure more fungi than flower.

And to me, a small caldera in the San Luis Valley
opens up like the petals of an golden-day lily,
an astronomer of the Milky Way
tracking of the phases of the moon,
the movement of the stars.

# Call to Action

Tracking the phases of the moon and the movement of the stars,
I will not be kidnapped
and ransomed, but posit a solution, document the obvious,
and make a nod to the alchemy of all our breaking hearts.
We need to turn our heads away from those who embrace
genocide and see the Earth as only commodity
or embellishment. Who have never visited African grasslands
or watched a walrus swim the Arctic Ocean, or chanced upon a herd
of elephants in the wild tending their young, or even seen
a hummingbird's nest. Or failed to hear the bird chorus
each morning outside their windows, or watched the seasonal drama
of maple groves in their cities.

Who do not have access to the mysterious
and are happy saying farewell to the northern white rhino
and ignore the genocide occurring in the Great Barrier Reef,
and celebrate subtractions, and call me a fool. I celebrate, instead,
the whole ecosystem from an archipelago of bees to pilot whales,
and the infinity of infinitesimal creatures,
each a hinge that stitches our home together. We are spun
from honey and blue butterflies on the mountains of Spain
and reject the Earth is soon-doomed. Just for the record,
there is an avalanche of data and evidence that cannot be ignored.
There is drought and wildfire. There is flooding and heat stroke deaths.
The planet is heating up and the teenagers are singing songs
to stranded whales.

# Bibliography

Burns, Ken. (director) *The American Buffalo*. (2023) Public Broadcasting System.

Debuys, William. *A Great Aridness: Climate Change and the Future of the American West*. Oxford University Press, Oxford, 2011.

Hornaday, William, T. *The Extermination of the American Bison*. Government Printing Office, Washington, D.C., 1889.

Ketcham, Chris. *This Land: How Cowboys, Capitalism, and Corruption are Ruining the American West*. Viking, New York, 2019.

Lippard, Lucy, R. *Undermining: A Wild Ride Through Land Use, Politics, and Art in the Changing West*. The New Press, London & New York, 2014.

Nash, Roderick Frazier. *Wilderness and the American Mind*. Yale University Press, New Haven & London, 2014.

Thompson, Jonathan. *River of Lost Souls: The Science, Politics and Greed Behind the Gold King Mine Spill*. Torrey House Press, Salt Lake City, 2018.

# Notes

## Utopia

### *Utopia*

"World Scientists' Warning of a Climate Emergency" Bioscience, Vol. 5.

Different sources suggest there are between 17-21 species of penguins, but, most agree there are 19 species of penguin.

## Renovation of the Human Race

The poems in this a series are mistranslations of Ovid's *Metamorphosis.* I used *The Hamilton, Lock and Clarke Series Selections from The Metamorphosees and Heriodes with an Interlinear Translation, for the Use of Schools and Private Learners, 1889,* a high school Latin textbook purchased at Goodwill in Denver, Colorado for a quarter. My translations were written in the margins and all over the text without regard to the original poems or any interest on my part of direct translations of Latin. The textbook served as a scaffold for my own poems.

*The Book of Symbols.* Editor-in-Chief, Ami Ronnberg. Taschen Books, 2010. The quote is from Paracelsus.

## The Colony

### *Livable Equilibrium*

"Nolan Doesken: Talking About the Weather with Colorado's State Climatologist" *Fort Collins Magazine,* Winter 2016.

### *What of the Honeybee?*
### *Once Royalty*

"Feds List 7 Hawaii Bee Species as Endangered, a first in US" Caleb Jones. AP News. September 30, 2016.

"For the First Time, Bees Declared Endangered in the United States." Christine Dell'Amore. *National Geographic,* October 2016.

*Dear Lucy—*

"Monarch Butterflies are Listed as an Endangered Species".
*Smithsonian Magazine.* 22 July 2022.

https://www.smithsonianmag.com/smart-news/migratory-monarch-butterflies-are-listed-as-an-endangered-species-180980461

Here is a recording of the migration of monarch butterflies in Mexico as they get ready for their annual migration.

https://mymodernmet.com/phil-torres-monarch-butterflies-recording

## Western Interior Seaway

### Uravan, Colorado

This poem relies heavily on "Uranium Widows" written by Peter Hessler and published in *The New Yorker.*

### Fracking

Just east of Fort Collins, Colorado, my home town, is the Niobrara Formation where over 50,000 sites dealing with all aspects of fracking exists.

### Sunset, Sangre de Cristo Mountains

Inspired by lines from Charles Simic and a six week camping trip in the Sangre de Cristo Mountains of southern Colorado.

## Megfauna

### Farewell, Sudan
### Captive Breeding

"Last Male Northern White Rhino Joins Tinder to Raise Money." BBC News. 25 April 2017.

"The Life He Lived: Photos of the Last Male Northern White Rhino. Written by Kyle Almond with photos by Amy Vitale. CNN. 18 February 2018.

https://www.cnn.com/interactive/2018/03/world/last-rhino-cnnphotos

Dvůr Králové Zoo is spearheading an international effort which includes the Ol Pejeta Conservancy in Kenya to save the northern white rhino, an animal I love unconditionally, by trying to produce the world's first test tube northern white baby rhino. Some progress is being made.

"Race Against Time to Prevent the Extinction of the Northern White Rhino." 17, February 2022.

https://safaripark.cz/en/conservation/northern-white-rhinos/biorescue-creates-two-new-embryos-in-race-against-time-to-prevent-the-extinction-of-the-northern-white-rhinoceros

The epicenter for conservation of the northern white rhino is Ol Pejeta Conservancy in Kenya, the current home of the last two northern white rhinos on the planet, Najin and Fatu.

https://www.olpejetaconservancy.org

A short video of the caretakers of Najin and Fatu, the last two northern white rhinos.

https://www.thedodo.com/videos/guy-takes-care-of-our-last-2-northern-white-rhinos

***On the Exhibition of a Rhinoceros at Venice by Pietro Longhi, 1751***

In 1751, a rhinoceros known as Miss Clara was captured in India and shipped to Europe. Miss Clara traveled for 17 years across Europe and inspired poems, paintings, tapestries, medals, sculptures and ladies to style their hair in the shape of a rhino horn.

### *Bison, bison*

William T. Horaday, the chief taxidermist of the National Musuem, believed because of hunting pressure, the bison was going to be extinct. He traveled to Mile City, Montana to collect specimens for museum display. He was so horrified by the slaughter of the bison, he dedicated the rest of his life to the saving the bison. He lobbied Congress and wrote *The Extermination of the America Bison,* a popular work that created public interest in saving the species.

*The Extemination of the American Bison* is available here:
https://www.gutenberg.org/files/17748

## Paradise
### *The Meadow Calls*

Inspired by Gregory Crewdson's series of stunning photographs documenting a single summer of the fireflies in a field outside   Pittsfield, Massachusetts. Featured at an exhibit at SITE: Santa Fe.

https://hyperallergic.com/128734/black-and-white-photographs-of-fireflies-lighting-up-summer-nightsr

### *I Turn Animal*

"25 Species, including the Pacific Walrus, Denied Endangered Protection by Trump Administration." Doyle Rice. *Washington Post*, 5 October 2017.

Endangered and Threatened Wildlife and Plants; 12-Month Findings on Petitions to List 25 Species as Endangered or Threatened Species. *The Federal Register: The Daily Journal of the United States Government.* The National Archives, 7 October, 2016.

# Acknowledgements

*Thank you to the following literary journals and publishers for first publishing these poems:*

"West Wind & West Fire" *Writing the West.*
American Museum of Western Art Denver, Colorado and the Rocky Mountain Land Library, Fairplay, Colorado.

"Notes Towards a Libretto (fig.3)" *Against Agamemnon: An Anthology of War Poetry.*

"Granite & Silver", "Cirque & Sky" & "Sagebrush & Mica" Colorado Art Share. Denver Botanic Gardens & Boulder Museum of Contemporary Art. Commissioned three letterpress broadsides printed by Wolverine Farm Publishing, Fort Collins, Colorado.

"Fracking" *Fort Collins Courier.*

Many of the poems first appeared in *Cirque & Sky*, winner of 2016 Middle Creek Publishing & Audio Fledge Chapbook Award.

## A Special Thank You

Thank you to my husband, Stephen Willard, for his unflinching support of my poetry for decades. All of my poems and all of my books would not be possible without his belief in my poetry.

Thank you, Amy Irish for all our past and future expeditions to open mics, poetry workshops and poetry festivals. You have enriched my poetry life.

Thank you, Dr. Elizabeth Cullen Dunn, writing partner and encourager of my work. You have been a keen reader and kind critic with an eye on always challenging me and pushing me in the right poetic direction.

Thank you, Carolyn Janeck for your topnotch, intuitive and transformative editing of all my poetry manuscripts.

Thank you, Wolverine Farm Poetry Group for the years and years of support of my poetry: Jack Martin, Lorrie Wolfe, Cecilia Turner, and Joan Welch.

Thank you, Todd Simmons of Wolverine Farm Publishing for your for continuously publishing my poems in *Matter, The Poetic Inventory of Rocky Mountain National Park* and the *Fort Collins Courier* and supporting my work a poet for many, many years.

Thank you, Joe Braun of Perlanda Books, curator of the best bookstore in the West, for spellbinding literary discussions, for allowing me to be a Reader-in-Residence at your bookstore twice and for your support of my poerty.

Thank you, Dan Beachy-Quick for being a champion of my poetry and for your continued support of my work.

A special thank you to Laura Mullen, my poetry professor at Colorado State University for teaching me to question everything in a poem, to experiment and loosen the boundaries of a poem, and liberate me as a poet.

My poetry flourishes with the support and guidance of all of you.

## About the Author:

**Kathleen Willard:**
Kathleen Willard has published four books including *The Next Noise Is Our Hearts* (2024), *This Incendiary Season* (2020), and *Cirque & Sky* (2016, Middle Creek Publishing & Audio), winner of the Fledge Chapbook Award, and *Electric Grace (2024, The Lune Press).*

Willard attended the Bread Loaf Writers Conference two times and the Disquiet International Literary Program in Lisbon, Portugal. She was awarded two artist residencies at Vermont Studio Center, a residency at Breckenridge Creative Arts Artist-in-Residence Program, and a residency at Mission Street Arts in Jemez, New Mexico. Three of her poems received Pushcart Prize nominations.

She received a National Endowment for the Humanities Fellowship to study the New England Renaissance which included travelling to New England and a Fulbright-Hays Fellowship to study in India. Many of her poems have been published in anthologies and literary magazines.

Willard publishes a newsletter called *Occasional Papers* focusing on literary subjects that strike her fancy and topics that she finds inspirational. To subscribe to *Occasional Papers,* email her at kathleen.d.willard@gmail.com Visit her website at www.kathleenwillard.com.

## About the Artist

**Johanna Mueller:**
Award winning printmaker, Johanna Mueller combines. the literary and mythical history of the animal with modern science to bring awareness of climate change, human encroachment on animal wilderness, and our overall need to preserve flora and fauna on this planet. Visit her website for more information about her work: www.johannamuellerprints.com

## About the Press

Middle Creek Publishing believes that responding to the world through art & literature—and sharing that response—is a vital part of being an artist.

Middle Creek Publishing is a company seeking to make the world a better place through both the means and ends of publishing. We are publishers of quality literature in any genre from authors and artists, both seasoned and those who are undiscovered or under-valued, or under-represented, with a great interest in works which illuminate or embody any aspect of contemplative Human Ecology, defined as the relationship between humans and their natural, social, and built environments.

Middle Creek Publishing's particular interest in Human Ecology is meant to clarify an aspect of the quality in the works we will consider for publication and as a guide to those considering submitting work to us. Our interest is in publishing works which illuminate the human experience through words, story or other content that connects us to each other, our environment, our history, and our potential deeply and more consciously.

www.ingramcontent.com/pod-product-compliance
Lightning Source LLC
Chambersburg PA
CBHW080734020726
47503CB00010B/2903